The Berenstain Bears'
NEW BABY

This way to Bear Country
You'll Know when You're there
As soon as you enter
You'll feel like a bear

A Random House PICTUREBACK®

The Berenstain Bears'

NEW BABY

Stan & Jan Berenstain

Random House New York

Down a sunny dirt road, over a log
bridge, up a grassy hill, deep in Bear
Country, lived a family of bears—
Papa Bear, Mama Bear and Small Bear.

They lived in a large tree
which Papa Bear had hollowed out
and made into a house.

It was a very fine house.
This is what it looked like inside.

It was fun growing up in Bear
Country...

helping Papa get honey from the old
bee tree...

helping Mama bring the vegetables
in from the garden.

There were all sorts of
interesting things for a
small bear to do and see
in Bear Country.

Small Bear felt good growing up
in a tree ... in his own room ... in the
snug little bed that Papa Bear had made
for him when he was a baby.

But one morning, it did not feel
so good. Small Bear woke up with
pains in his knees and aches in his legs.

"Small Bear, you have outgrown
your little bed," said Papa Bear, as he
hitched up his overalls and buttoned
his shoulder straps.

"Today, we shall go out into the woods and make you a bigger one!"

With that, he ate his
breakfast of piping-hot
porridge . . .

washed it down with a
gulp of honey from the
family honey pot . . .

took up his ax and was
out the door.

"But, Papa," called
Small Bear, following
after him. "What will
happen to my little bed?"

"Don't worry about that,
Small Bear," said Mama Bear
as she closed the door after him.

She smiled and patted her
front, which had lately grown
very big and round.
   "You've outgrown
that snug little bed
just in time!"

"What will happen to my little bed?" Small Bear asked as he caught up with Papa Bear. But Papa was sharpening his ax on his grinding stone and didn't hear.

"Yes, indeed," said Papa Bear. "You need a bed you can stretch out in—a bed that will not give you pains in your knees and aches in your legs."

He tested
the ax to see
if it was sharp,

then headed off
into the woods.

"What will happen to my little bed?"
Small Bear asked again as he caught up with
Papa Bear in the woods. Papa had chopped
down a tree and was splitting it into boards.
"We will have a new baby soon
who will need that little bed,"
said Papa Bear as he whacked
off another board.

"A new baby?" asked Small Bear.
(He hadn't noticed that Mama Bear had
grown very round lately, although he
had noticed it was harder and harder
to sit on her lap.)

"And it's coming soon?"

"Yes, *very* soon!" said Papa Bear.

With a final whack he split off the last
board, which gave him enough wood to make
a bigger bed for Small Bear.

They made the bed a good size
and took the rest of the day to
chip and shave it smooth and neat.
Then they carried it back to
the tree and up to Small Bear's room.

When they got there,
Small Bear noticed right away
that his old bed wasn't there
any more.

"My little bed!" said
Small Bear. "It's already
gone!"

"You outgrew it just in time,"
called Mama Bear from the next room.
"Come and see."

It was true! There was his snug
little bed with a new little baby in it.
Small Bear had outgrown his snug
little bed just in time for his new baby
sister. And now *he* was a *big brother!*

She was very little but very
lively. As Small Bear leaned over
for a closer look, she popped him
on the nose with a tiny fist.

"Hmm," said Small Bear. "She has a pretty good punch for a little baby."

That night he stretched out
proudly in his bigger bed.
"Aah!" he said. "Being a
big brother is going to be fun."

The next morning he woke up feeling fine,
with no pains in his knees or aches in his legs.
His nose was a little tender, though.